THE SUMMER UNPLUGGED SERIES

BOOK 4

SPRING UNLEASHED

AMY SPARLING

WITHDRAWN

Cover image from shutterstock.com
First Edition March 1st, 2014

CHAPTER 1

My name echoes through the small auditorium of my high school. I'm surprised I hear Principal Walsh's voice over the thumping of my heart inside of my chest. I take a few steps forward, graduation gown swishing around my legs and just a tiny bit too long for comfort. If I tripped and fell right now I would be so mortified. This isn't like falling in the hallway or something—it would be falling in front of the entire senior class and their families.

Luck is on my side though, because soon I'm right in front of Principal Walsh and he's handing me a fake diploma because they mail out the real ones and he's shaking my hand and I don't even screw up the handshake like I had worried about for the last three days. I can't stop the massive grin on my face as I walk off stage and join the rest of my graduated classmates back in the folded metal chairs at the front of the room.

I did it. I am officially finished with high school.

Somewhere in the audience behind me is my mom and my little brother Bentley. Mom's probably swatting away tears of pride and Bentley is no doubt bored out of his mind and wishing he had his Nintendo DS to keep him company.

The person sitting next to my brother is the one I can't keep my mind off of. Jace Adams. My super-hot and always wonderful boyfriend of eleven months and sixteen days. I don't normally pay attention to how many days we've been together, but our one year anniversary is coming up quickly and I am just as excited about it as I am about finally graduating high school.

I am eighteen, I am no longer tied to eight hours of school every day and I have almost been Jace's girlfriend for an entire year. My life seriously can't get any better than this. I know it's pathetic, but I feel my cheeks turning red at the thought of Jace sitting somewhere in the audience behind me. I miss him so much even though we're in the same room together. Unfortunately I have to wait until graduation is over so I can run and find him and my family in the crowd. It's only a few minutes away, but it'll feel like an eternity.

A set of long brown curls swooshes around from the seat in front of me and Becca, my best friend, gives me a quick smile and a thumbs up. I had confided in her before the ceremony that I was terrified of tripping and eating the stage when I walked up to accept my diploma. So her silly little thumbs up is probably her way of congratulating me on not embarrassing the hell out of myself. I give her a thumbs up in return and sink back in my chair, letting myself get consumed in thoughts of Jace until the ceremony is over.

Mom takes everyone out to a celebratory dinner after graduation and her boyfriend surprises me by paying for the entire meal. Mom was single for pretty much all of my life and it's really awesome seeing her so happy now. Plus Jace and I think that her newfound lovesickness has changed her personality in ways that benefit us. She used to hate the idea of dating and wouldn't want me to do anything with a guy. Now she encourages my relationship—of course, Jace's freaking perfect personality probably helps with winning her over.

Jace grabs my hand the moment we say goodbye to my family in the restaurant parking lot. I wrap my other hand around his arm and snuggle close to him as we walk to his truck.

"So how does it feel to be an alumnus of Lawson High?" he asks after he places a quick kiss on the top of my head.

"It hasn't really sunken in yet." I roll my eyes in a playful way when Jace pops open the passenger door for me. Ever since I poked fun of him for being too much of a Southern Gentleman, he's made it a point to open my door all the time. Even when we just take a quick trip to the gas station or something lame. I love it though, secretly, but I still make fun of him. I crawl up into my side of his truck and lean over to accept the kiss he plants on my lips before closing my door. Even after eleven months and sixteen days, the boy still gives me butterflies.

Jace gets in his truck and starts the engine. "I'm sure it'll sink in soon. High school students don't get to go to parties on a Thursday night," he says, alluding to Becca's graduation party that we're on our way to, "But a graduated person can party whenever they want."

"Woohoo," I say with a laugh. "You know, this is like the first party we've ever been to together."

"Really? Yeah I guess you're right," he says, crumpling up his eyebrows as he thinks. "Guess we'll have to make it extra fun." He wiggles his eyebrows in a sinister yet playful way. I look out the window so he doesn't see me blush.

Becca's mom works for a lawyer and he owns a beach house off the coast of Lawson on one of those exclusive private beaches on the east end of town. She managed to talk him into letting her throw a small get-together for Becca and her friends for graduation. A get-together is what we're supposed to call it, as her mom emphasized a million times while Becca and I were handwriting invitations for the party. She said if her boss thought it would be a *party* then he wouldn't allow it. When we arrive at the address, we have to park on the side of the road three houses down.

I'm guessing her boss would flip if he saw how many cars were here. "I didn't know Becca had this many friends," I say as we make our way up the sandy roadside toward the beach house. Jace nods and wraps an arm around me. "With that girl's annoying laugh, I figured you were her *only* friend."

"Be nice." I elbow him in the ribs but I can't keep a serious face because Becca's laugh is pretty awful. Luckily her personality makes up for it.

Music blasts through the house, audible from outside. We make our way up the two flights of stairs to the balcony that provides a beautiful view of the ocean in front of us. Only about twenty people our age are here but I guess they all decided to drive themselves instead of carpooling. Can't say I blame them…if I had a car I would want to drive everywhere as well.

I pull Jace to the edge of the balcony so we can spend a quiet moment taking in the gorgeous view of the water as the sun begins to set. Eventually I want to find Becca and get our party on, but right now I'm happy just spending time leaning against the wooden railing, feeling Jace's strong chest press against my back.

Our peaceful moment lasts about thirty seconds.

"Girl! You told me he was hot, but you didn't tell me he was this hot!" I cringe inwardly as I turn to face Becca's mom.

"Hi Ms. Gina," I say, twisting to the side as Jace takes one preventative step backward. He can spot a cougar a mile away, the poor thing. But it's not their fault he's so freaking hot. "This is Jace, my boyfriend," I say by way of introduction.

She steps forward, pushing her bleach blonde hair behind her ears and grabs his outstretched hand with both of hers. The stench of liquor on her breath hits me like a punch in the face. "I've heard all about you," she says, letting her eyes wander over Jace's muscular frame. I'm surprised he doesn't wince in pain from her super long acrylic nails stabbing into his skin. He's such a nice guy though. All he does is smile and thank her.

Becca rushes up, red plastic cup in her hand. "Mom!" she grabs her mom's elbow and pulls her back. "Don't harass Bayleigh and Jace."

Ms. Gina rolls her eyes in an overdramatic way. "She's so embarrassed of her momma," she says, dismissing Becca's mortification with a wave of her hand. "Ya'll come get some food and drinks. Have fun." She smiles at me and winks at Jace. "Come get me if you need anything, ya hear?"

Becca watches her mom disappear back into the beach house and then she turns to me. "This is like the coolest graduation party ever, but having my mom here kind of ruins the fun."

I shrug. "You get used to her. And your party rocks."

"This is a great view," Jace says, motioning to the beach below. A pink flash flies through the air and I notice there's a game of beach volleyball going on below us with a hot pink ball.

Becca's face falls when Jace speaks, as if she'd forgotten he was also here. "Well, I'm sure this is nothing compared to all the parties you've been to."

He shakes his head. "Rich people parties are overrated. I'd rather be here with my girl and her friends."

We stuff ourselves with the delicious array of finger foods displayed on three large tables in the living room. Becca's mom pulled out all the stops for this party—there's copious amounts of food and sparkly decorations all over the place.

When my stomach is full and I've chatted with all of our mutual friends who came to the party, Jace and I sink into a fluffy couch that's located in the...well I'm not sure what room it is. Beach houses are weird. When we entered the house from the porch, we were in a massive entertaining area with food and drinks. To the left is an entrance to what I'd consider a living room because it has a couch and a big screen TV. But off to the side of the room, next to the entire wall of windows is a massive built in hot tub. Like, the floor suddenly turns into a hot tub. Inside the house.

"Beach houses are weird," I say aloud to Jace as we watch the bubbles rise up from the empty hot tub.

"They aren't usually weird, but this one is." He glances behind us and then back at me. "We should lock that door and then jump in."

"We don't have any bathing suits," I say, completely missing the silly eyebrow wiggle he directs to me. He leans in close and whispers, "We don't need a bathing suit."

Chills run down my spine at the mention of skinny dipping with Jace in someone else's house. Of course we can't actually do it, we would totally get caught by the tons of people hanging out in the house. Since Jace is so close, I lean forward to kiss him. "I wish we could," I say.

He smiles. "One day we'll get a ridiculous beach house and we'll put two hot tubs in the living room."

"I'd like that very much."

"Really? You don't seem like a two hot dub kind of girl."

I roll my eyes. "Oh I'm sorry, have we never talked about my hot tub preferences? Maybe we weren't in as serious of a relationship as I thought we were."

He playfully pokes his finger in my ribs. "Baby you can have as many hot tubs as you want."

I sit up straight and cross my arms over my chest. "That's more like it. But it doesn't really matter because we don't live together." I end the sentence with my lips in a pout. Moving in with Jace is a sensitive topic for me. Ever since the day I turned eighteen last winter I've wanted to move in with him. Mom and Jace made me finish high school first. Well, they didn't *make* me. I wanted to finish school. But you know…in a perfect world a girl wouldn't have to wait to do anything when it comes to being with the man she loves.

But now school is officially over and no one has said a word about what we'll do next. Not Mom, not Jace, and not me because I'm too timid about it. I can't just force my way into living with Jace. I'd like him to *ask* me first.

I'm just not sure he ever will.

"What's that look for?" Jace asks, furrowing his eyebrows as he looks at me.

Guess I had been lost in my thoughts and they had taken over my facial expression. I take a deep breath and give him a small smile. "Nothing, I'm fine."

CHAPTER 2

My mom's boyfriend David sings along with the opening theme song on a Disney channel show my brother watches every morning. The silly melody is the first thing I hear when I leave my bedroom the next day. David's terrible singing voice isn't what makes me want to barf before I've even eaten breakfast. It's his wardrobe.

When head down the stairs and round the corner into the kitchen, my mouth watering with the smell of pancakes and bacon cooking on the stove, I come face to face with David's baggy black sweatpants and oversized orange t-shirt with the sleeves cut out. I'm talking cut out so deep that I can see his ribcage and the side of his man boobs. It's the kind of shirt he wears to the gym to work out but should never, ever, be worn to cook breakfast.

I have got to get out of this place. I like David and all, but…gross.

He does make a great breakfast, but so does Jace. I'd way rather wake up to the sound of Jace singing along with stupid cartoons. Of course, I have no idea why Jace would be watching Disney cartoons at nine in the morning. I shake my head to clear it of these idiotic thoughts and get back to thoughts that actually count: figuring out my plan to live with Jace.

After saying goodbye to him last night, I had lain awake in bed before falling asleep, thinking about my future and how to make it all work out in the end. It took a while for me to stop being annoyed that Jace insisted on going home after Becca's party. We got back to my house around midnight and Mom would have let him stay over since it was so late, but he just had to make the forty-five minute drive home for whatever reason.

It's the "reasons" that bothered me so much. He claimed he had "things" and "stuff" to do in the morning. His vagueness wouldn't have bothered me if it were a weekday because he has a busy and complicated job, but ever since Jace and I have become more serious in our relationship, he's scheduled his work on weekdays only so as to keep weekends free for me. And today is a Saturday, dammit. What could he possibly be doing?

I didn't ask though, because I don't want to be the annoying, nagging girlfriend. I want to be the awesome girlfriend who isn't a jealous freak and who is a delight to be around. Jace always calls me his ray of sunshine and that's all I want to be for him. So instead of pressing the issue and asking to know what kind of things he could possibly be busy with today, I just let it go.

And then I obsessed over them alone in my bed after he went home like the weirdo I am.

I have bigger problems right now than wondering what Jace is doing today. Monday will be my first weekday as an adult and I'm realizing what a total loser I have become in just twenty four hours after graduating high school. When I was a student, that's all I had to worry about. Now I'm an adult and I'm a total embarrassment. I have no job and I'm not in college.

Becca took a job as a cashier at the local pharmacy and plans to work all summer before starting community college in the fall. She had offered to let me go job hunting with her a month ago but I turned in down out of wanting to spend more time with Jace. It seemed like a good idea at the time. Now I feel like the world's biggest loser.

Mom's been pressuring me to go to college but no matter how many times I look over the degree list, nothing jumps out at me as being career-worthy. It's painfully embarrassing to admit it to myself, but for the last year of my life, all I want to do is be with my love. I know it's stupid and I know that love is just love. It doesn't put food on the table or a shelter over our heads. That doesn't stop me from knowing that I'm in love and have found my soul mate. But I can't keep living my life only caring about spending time with Jace. I have to grow up.

That's pretty much the conclusion I came to last night before finally drifting into a restless sleep. I try to suppress a yawn but it's no use. David hands me a plate and I load up some pancakes and bacon and then join Bentley at the table. Mom is still in the shower which is great because she's the only chatty one in the mornings. The rest of us are content to eat our food quietly in our half-awake stupor.

I mull over the worries in my mind, trying to come up with a plan for my future. It hurts to think of this, but maybe the reason Jace hasn't talked to me about moving in with him is because I am a massive loser. I don't have a job to help contribute with the bills and I don't have a car even if I did have a job. I'm not in school and again, even if I was in school, I still have no car to get to classes every day.

It's no wonder Jace doesn't want me to live with him. I'd just be a worthless liability. Jace insists on paying for our dinner and picking up the bill when we do fun thinks like ice skating or go to the movies. I always thought it was because he was just being romantic, but what if deep down he secretly resents me for it? I don't want to be someone's liability.

I have to get a job and I have to prove to him and to my mom and everyone else that I am not a big loser with no future. I stab into a piece of pancake and shove it in my mouth and think up a game plan. Mom and David plan on going shopping today so hopefully Mom will let me use her car while they're gone. I'll go to the mall first and ask every single business if they're hiring. Then I'll stop in every store within a five mile range and apply for jobs. That way I can find a job that's close enough for me to ride my bike to if I can't get a ride from anyone. I'll try to schedule working hours in the daytime so Jace and I will still have evenings together.

By the time Mom enters the kitchen wearing pajamas and a towel on her head, I'm already feeling pretty confident about my plans for the day. I'll stop by at least two dozen businesses and one of them has to be hiring. I won't even tell anyone what I'm doing until after I get a job offer. Mom and Jace will be proud of me.

I smile brightly at Mom when she tells us good morning. Today will be a good day. "Good morning, Mom. Can I borrow the car today?"

She doesn't even look me in the eye. "No, honey."

My fork drops to my plate. "Why not? I thought you and David were going shopping? He always takes his truck, so…"

She nods. "We are going shopping but you can't take my car. Sorry."

"Why?" I ask, trying not to sound so annoyed, but I know it doesn't work.

Mom gives me a warning glare as my only answer. Ugh. I pick up my fork and take another bite so my mouth isn't free to talk because the only words I can think of will get me in trouble. I don't want to be a jerk right now, but I desperately need the car to fulfill my mission. I guess I'll have to tell her my mission so she'll let me use the car. It'll be no fun surprising her with the news that I got a job when she already knows I'm looking for one.

I swallow and take a deep breath. "I'll just have to find another way, I guess."

"Another way to do what?" Mom asks curiously.

I shrug and take a while to answer since I know I've piqued her interest. "Oh I just had something important to do, and I really needed the car…but I guess I'll survive on my bike instead."

David lets out a little snort of laughter, which takes a lot of energy for me to ignore. Mom shakes her head. "I'm afraid you won't be doing anything this morning, Bayleigh."

Okay now I'm really pissed off. "Why do you say that?" I ask, mentally picking up and dusting off my *I'm eighteen and I can do what I want card* just in case I have to use it.

Before she can answer me, the doorbell rings. The four of us turn toward the door and Bentley jumps off his barstool, screaming "I'll get it! I'll get it!" as he runs to the living room. Mom stands as well, placing her fork on her plate and taking one long sip of her coffee. She nods toward the front door. "That's why."

I hear Jace's voice before I see him, and then I see his hand reach out and rub the top of my little brother's head. "What's going on, little man?" he says as Bentley lets him inside the house.

Three things run through my mind at the same time: ridiculously huge amounts of excitement that Jace is here, annoyance at my mother for knowing he was coming over and not telling me, and then a horrendous embarrassment at the realization that I'm wearing ugly pajamas, my hair is unwashed and in a messy bun and my eyes probably look like raccoons from the eye makeup I totally didn't wash off last night. I had gotten home so late, all I had the energy to do was fall face forward in my bed, despite staying up late, deep in thought.

"Oh my god," I say as I bury my face in my hands. When I slowly lift my head again, Jace hovers in front of me with a big smile on his face. David small talks to him about motocross and the professional race that's coming to town next month. I really wish Jace would look at David as they talk, but instead, he keeps sneaking glances at me. I climb off my stool and rush to Jace's side, throwing my arms around his rib cage and pressing my face against his side. Now I can hug him and he doesn't exactly get to see my ugly morning face.

"You're a little early," Mom says. "Would you like some coffee?"

"Sure, I could use it," Jace replies as his fingers wrap around my side.

"Would somebody please tell me what's going on here?" I ask, looking from my boyfriend to my mom, temporarily forgetting to hide my gross face.

Jace lets a smirk slip out from under his coffee mug. "I don't know what you're talking about," he says, glancing sideways at Mom who has an equally sneaky grin on her face.

"Guys, this isn't funny. What are you keeping from me?"

Jace sets down the mug and reaches into his pocket, grabbing his keys. He tosses them a few inches in the air and catches them. "You're wrong, babe. I think it is very funny." He tosses the keys up and catches them a few more times.

David laughs. "Yeah, it's definitely funny."

I look from my boyfriend to my family and back again. "Fine, don't tell me," I say giving Jace a little shove that almost makes him drop his keys. Only...wait, those aren't his keys. His keys have a tiny metal dirt bike keychain on them. I grab the keys out of his palm. It's one single car key with a pink sparkly keychain attached. The keychain is the initial B.

…for Bayleigh?

"Who's car is this?" I ask.

Mom clasps her hands together in front of her chest as she bounces on her heels. "It's yours," she squeals as if she might burst from holding in the information any longer.

A flash of confusion hits me, followed by excitement. Total chaos erupts as I take one look at Jace and then bolt to the front door. The whole family follows me as I dive off the porch and stop suddenly in the middle of the grass when I see my new car.

A pearly blue, extra shiny Chevrolet Cobalt with a big pink bow on the hood. I'm transfixed for a few moments, unable to move or think clearly as I put the pieces together.

"That bow was a nice touch," Mom tells Jace. "Good job."

I look back to see them high-five each other and that's when I finally get my voice again. "*You*." I point at my boyfriend. "You were in on this! How did you keep this a secret from me?"

He smiles. "Some secrets are worth it."

Bentley runs his fingers over the pink bow, his mouth open in childlike wonder at how a bow could be so huge. Mom comes forward and wraps her arm around my shoulders. "How do you like your graduation present?"

"Mom, I can't believe this," I say, lowering my voice for the next part. "You don't have the money for this kind of gift."

"We all pitched in," she says, glancing back at Jace and David. "All of us."

Chills prickle over my arms. I can't believe everyone cares about me enough to do this. "Thanks, you guys. This is amazing."

We all take turns playing with the car, sitting in the driver's seat and checking out all the features. Mom takes pictures of Bentley while he pretends to drive the car despite his feet not being able to touch the pedals. Jace grabs my hand and brings it to his lips. "I love you, Bay."

"I love you, too." Being next to him brings a sense of peace over my body, smoothing over all my anxiety from last night. Realization hits me as I remember my restless sleep. "This is what you meant when you said you had things to do this morning. I thought you just didn't want to hang out with me."

"Psh." Jace rolls his eyes. "I always want to hang out with you. Like I said, some secrets are worth keeping. Oh yeah," he says, scratching the back of his neck. "Um, I kind of need a ride home."

"Oh my god I'm so excited," I say, bouncing on my heels. "I just realized that I'll get to go visit you now. You don't always have to come get me anymore."

Mom clears her throat. "Jace…did you not talk to her yet?"

I glance at Jace just in time to see him cringe. "I thought you were going to talk to her."

CHAPTER 3

Bentley yells my name from twenty feet in the air. I look up and see his chubby face squished into the hole in a red tube at the McDonald's Play Place. "This is so cool," he squeals before ducking back into the tubing and disappearing amongst all the other kids. Jace and I brought him to lunch with us since Mom and David are shopping for patio furniture and being drug around from store to store is considered pure torture to a third grader.

I sip on my milkshake and watch the energetic blobs of children race through the ball pit and climb up to the slides. I never know where Bentley is at any given time because his messy hair blends in with everyone else's kid.

"You're being quiet," Jace says, leaning back in a swivel chair. His foot rocks him slowly from left to right. As his fingers rest in his lap, intertwining with each other, I find myself fascinated with the veins in his forearms. "Like, quieter than I've ever seen you." He reaches up and pokes me. "I'm not even entirely sure if you're conscious or not."

I pull my gaze away from his sexy arms and shrug. "I'm not being quiet."

He slides back in his chair, pulling his arms up and lacing his fingers behind his head. He is so ridiculously sexy in this position and all I want to do is throw myself on his lap. Too bad there are a dozen kids and their parents around. Jace is hell-bent on continuing to talk even though I'm content with sitting quietly. "I kind of thought we'd be talking about the situation now."

The *situation*, as he calls it, is the weird offer my mother presented to me this morning, after Jace revealed that he hadn't talked to me about it. Apparently my boyfriend and mother have schemed against me, talked behind my back and without my knowledge and came up with what Mom considers a *great* plan for my future. That plan involves me signing up for Brazos Community College in exchange for Mom's permission to move in with Jace.

Yeah. Talk about making me want to crawl into a hole and die. My mother called Jace a week before graduation and basically backed him into a corner, telling him she knows I'm planning on moving in with him this summer. The thing is, I totally wasn't planning on it! I mean, I was, but I hadn't told Jace about it yet. I was still holding out hope that he would ask me to move in instead of me asking him if I could. And I sure as hell hadn't told my mother about it. I guess she just guessed what my intentions were, and unfortunately for me, she guessed right.

Now I'm humiliated beyond repair. I'm not exactly mad at Jace for taking her call and hearing what she had to say. It wasn't his fault that she contacted him like that. But I'm upset and I feel betrayed that he didn't tell me the moment it happened. When they sat me down in the kitchen after giving me my car this morning, Mom told me all about her plan and Jace just sat there and listened with me. I kept watching his facial expressions to see if he didn't want me to move in with him, but he was a blank slate.

Anyway, I don't want to go to college. I don't want my mother telling me what to do. And in case she forgot, I am eighteen now and I sure as hell don't need her permission to move away from home. Of course, I don't want her to hate me either. Now I'm stuck with some stupid plan my mom made for me, and a boyfriend who hasn't implicitly told me if he's okay with it or not. Hell, I'm not even okay with it.

So when Jace tells me I'm being quiet, I don't even know what to say.

"Sorry," eventually comes out of my mouth.

"You don't need to be sorry, babe." Jace waves at Bentley, who has his hand shoved through the netting in the ball pit, waving at us. "I understand that the kids' area of a McDonald's isn't exactly the best place to discuss our future. I'm just anxious for your decision."

"*My* decision?" I snap. "I don't think you and Mom left me room to make a decision."

"Baby, don't be like that. This is your life. It's our life. What you want matters."

I fold my arms over my chest. "Then why is my mother involved?"

Bentley reeks of sweat as he comes crashing into me a split second later, knocking the breath out of me. He crawls into my lap and grabs a handful of fries. "Those boys keep using the slide over and over," he grumbles, shooting a glare toward a group of older kids who probably shouldn't be on the playground at all.

"Want me to beat them up?" Jace asks. Bentley breaks into an evil smile but then shakes his head. "I don't want you to get in trouble."

Jace smiles at me and I smile back, our universal gesture for *This isn't over yet, but we can't talk about it now*. That's fine with me, of course. I'm not sure I want to talk about it at all.

CHAPTER 4

The sound of whipped cream spraying out of an aerosol can makes me turn away from the first episode of Supernatural on the television. It's Monday afternoon and Becca and I have decided to spend our summer rewatching all of our favorite shows from start to finish. She doesn't know that I might be moving out soon, and at this point I'm not even sure if I know what my plans are. The frothy sound comes again and I glare at her.

"You're holding out on me, jerk." I laugh and steal the can of whipped cream from her. She nods to the fabric shopping bag she brought over from her house. "There's another can in there. I know I can't trust you to use it sparingly. I also brought sprinkles?" she says as if it's a question. "I'm not sure if we're too old for sprinkles on our ice cream now."

I dig into the bag of ice cream and syrup toppings, pull out a plastic jar of heart shaped sprinkles and scatter them on top of my oversized bowl of ice cream. "If we ever get too old for sprinkles I want you to kill me."

Becca rolls her eyes and settles next to me on the massive bean bag couch in front of the television in my room. "Yeah right. If I killed you then Jace would kill me."

As we settle in to watch our show, I eat my ice cream and try to think of a way to bring up the stuff I need to talk about with my best friend. The whole moving in with Jace thing and the college thing and the stupid nagging in the pit of my stomach that's telling me he doesn't want me living with him since he never actually asked.

This whole past weekend was muted with my feelings of worry and anger with my mom for letting Jace in on a matter that should have been a private one between him and me. It was, hands down, my least favorite weekend with my boyfriend. Nothing was bad— we didn't argue or anything—but I just felt like a total loser around him. I kept waiting for him to ask me to move in and he never did. Just the thought of bringing up this subject with Becca makes me lower my head and dive my spoon back into the ice cream.

Becca interrupts my thoughts with one of her own. "One thing we have to do this summer is throw some kick ass parties at your boyfriend's apartment."

"Definitely," I say with a smile. "If I get my way, I won't ever be leaving his apartment."

Becca's eyes widen. "Are you moving in with him?"

I shrug. Now is as good of time as any to tell her about my situation with Mom and Jace. Becca's expression flickers from surprise to mortification as I tell her about my secret desires to have Jace ask me to live with him and how Mom totally ruined it by getting to him before I did and demanding that I attend college.

"That is so rude and annoying," Becca says after my ten minute long rant on my mother. "You're a legal adult now. I can't believe she would butt into your life like that."

"TELL ME ABOUT IT," I say before instantly realizing that Mom might hear me from the other room if I don't stay quiet. "It was so embarrassing! Jace and I haven't even had the official talk about moving in yet." I run my hands through my hair, balling them into fists at the back of my head. "We have had talks about how I'm free to stay with him whenever I want to. Plus I have a lot of my stuff at his place already. I just can't believe my freaking mother beat him to it before I did."

"Don't get pissed at me for saying this," Becca begins, "But why don't you just go to community college and move in with Jace? I mean, I don't even understand why you refuse to go to college in the first place."

My shoulders sag as I let out an exhausted sigh. "Because I'm not smart, Becca! I can't take stupid college classes. I suck at math and would have to take remedial courses before I can even take the ones you get credit for." I lower my forehead into my hands and stare at the carpet below my feet. "Jace doesn't have a college degree and he does just fine."

Becca places a reassuring hand on my arm. "Not everything requires lots of math classes. Do what I'm doing and get a certification for something."

"Yeah, maybe," I say just to shut her up about it. I know that college is important for a lot of people but it isn't important for me. All I want is a fun job that makes me happy. One that doesn't require math. If only there were paid professions that involved watching Jace work in the hot sun with his shirt off at the motocross track. Hey, a girl can dream.

"So how's the fancy new car?" Becca asks during a particularly boring part of the episode where Sam and Dean aren't on screen.

"It's pretty amazing but I'm starting to wonder how I'll ever fill it up with gas or pay the insurance without a freaking job." Yeah, job searching was promptly put on hold since Jace was with me all weekend. Guess I should start looking first thing tomorrow morning.

"I wish you would come get a job at the pharmacy," Becca says. "We're still hiring and you and I could totally work the same shift together."

"But it's the evening shift," I whine and reach for the can of whipped cream. "Evenings are the only time I can hang out with Jace."

"Blah blah blah," she says, flapping her fingers and thumb as if they were my mouth. "I'm Bayleigh and all I care about is my hot famous boyfriend."

"You're damn right I do," I say as I toss my head back and empty the rest of the whipped cream into my mouth.

"My college classes don't start until August but even I know that shit will rot your teeth," Becca says as she watches me look like a chipmunk with my cheeks stuffed with delicious sugary goodness. She's studying to be a dental hygienist and I am so not ready to be lectured by her.

I point my spoon at her in an accusatory way. "If you're suddenly all about dental health then why did you bring over this bag full of cavity causers?"

She shrugs. "Bayleigh, do you think I'm too bossy?"

I lift an eyebrow and look away from the television. "No, I knew you were joking about the teeth thing just now."

She shakes her head. "No, I know. I just mean in general. Am I a bossy, nagging bitch? Do I think I'm better than everyone else and use my supposed superiority to look down on others?"

I grab the remote and press the pause button, causing the characters on screen to freeze while in the middle of a life-threatening fight. "Where the hell did that come from?"

She looks at her hands and shakes her head. "It seems like every guy I date ends up telling me that at some point in our relationship. Do you remember Blake?"

I nod. How could I not remember Blake? He's a year older than us and up until two weeks ago, he and Becca were in the tangled web of sort-of-dating-sort-of-not-dating. She got so sick of me asking what was up with them that I finally just let it go, despite being desperate to know what happened. The dejected look on my best friend's face tells me that I finally get to discover why they quit talking.

"I thought things with Blake were good and that they were moving in the right direction. I mean, I thought he would ask me to be his official girlfriend any day and then he just blew up at me and yelled that I'm too pushy and intrusive and bossy." She takes a deep breath and stares at the paused screen on the television. "I don't know why I can't keep a freaking boyfriend. Hell, I can't even get a boyfriend. Apparently I'm good enough to have sex with but not good enough to be in a relationship with."

I slide over on the massive bean bag and lay my head on her shoulder. I've known Becca long enough to know that she doesn't like making eye contact when she's upset about something. "What happened to make him blow up at you?" I ask. I'm not exactly an expert at relationships but maybe I can help her figure out what went wrong.

"I don't want to talk about it," she mumbles.

"Nope," I snap. "You do not get to bring up a subject like this and then not talk about it, missy."

She snorts at my stupid nickname and shakes her head. "It's embarrassing and stupid and I don't want to tell you."

"Okay now you have to tell me."

She shakes her head again. I lift my head and turn toward her, putting on my pretend serious face. Except I suck at looking serious so it's really just an expression of me holding back laughter while staring wide-eyed at her. "Don't make me kick your ass. Tell me what happened."

She lets out a sigh and plays with the drawstring on her pajama shorts. "Fine. Just...don't make fun of me."

I roll my hand, signaling for her to continue. She takes a deep breath. "Blake was just like every other asshole guy and he had a lock on his cell phone. I hate how they do that. He claimed he didn't have anything to hide and that he wasn't dating anyone else, but if you have nothing to hide then you don't need a password, you know?"

I nod, mentally wondering if Jace has a lock on his phone. I don't remember ever paying attention to it. "So what happened?"

Clearly something happened, because she looks really freaking embarrassed. Her fingers twine together and she stares at her lap the entire time she talks. "It really bothered me that he would get a ton of text messages when we were together, and it just seemed like such a hassle to type in the four digit code to open his phone and read the text each time. I started getting like, obsessed with figuring out his code. I didn't think I'd actually snoop through his phone but…I don't know, maybe I would. So started watching when he typed his code and I finally figured it out. It was zero four zero one which is his birthday."

"Did you find something bad on his phone?" I ask. She shakes her head.

"I never got that far. One day he got a text and it made him laugh when he read it, so I kind of hovered next to him trying to seem casual so I could peek at who was texting him. Well when he went to unlock his phone again, the code wasn't the usual numbers he always did so, like a freaking idiot, I blurted out, 'Hey you changed your lock code.'"

My lips squish to the side of my mouth. "Uh oh."

She bites her lip and nods. "Yeah. It was bad. He got really pissed and accused me of spying on him. Then he said I was too bossy and intrusive and that this is why he didn't want to date me because I was a shitty person who wanted to control him."

"Becca, I'm sorry." I try to picture the scenario she just explained. Other guys from my past, like Ian, probably would have reacted the same way. But when I mentally put Jace into that situation, I can't see the same outcome. Jace doesn't yell at me like that.

Becca sets her empty ice cream bowl on the floor and rolls herself out of the bean bag. Her hands rest on her hips as she walks to my bedroom window and stares out of it, deep in thought. "I bet Chase wouldn't react like that," she says, referring to my neighbor whose bedroom window is visible from her viewpoint. She's had a crush on him since he moved in last winter, but he doesn't feel the same way about her. She throws her hands up in frustration. "Who am I kidding? I bet he would. All guys are assholes and they're all so damn secretive with their stupid phones. I guess I should just get over it if I ever want to have a boyfriend."

"You'll find someone who isn't an asshole," I say, wishing I had better words to comfort her. A year and a month ago before I met Jace, I might have felt the same way in thinking that all guys were jerks. But I got lucky enough to find my soul mate and I know Becca will too.

"How do you manage it?" Becca turns toward me, her hands still on her hips. "How do you put up with never knowing who Jace is talking to or what kind of secrets he keeps on his phone?"

I shrug. "I never thought about it. He doesn't keep secrets from me."

Becca lets out a snort of laughter. "Wow, Bay. That's like the biggest lie ever." My eyebrows shoot up in surprise at her accusation and she quickly adds, "I mean, I love Jace. I totally do. But you can't say he doesn't keep secrets from you. He's just another guy, after all."

Now *my* hands are on my hips. I'm trying not to get offended because I know she's just mad at her own situation, but it's hard not to want to take someone's head off when they insult my boyfriend. "I have no reason to think that he keeps secrets from me. He tells me everything."

"Really?" Her voice drips with sarcasm. "Remember just a few months ago when you were constantly freaking out about his Facebook and all those parties he went to and all the girls he took pictures with? You can't possibly think that there aren't any questionable text messages on his phone he doesn't want you to know about."

"Well I sure as hell didn't snoop through his phone to find out," I say, entirely too defensively as I sink back into the bean bag. The reason I never snooped through his phone was because the idea didn't occur to me. I'm not an obsessive phone-snooper like Becca is. A lump forms in my throat.

Jace doesn't keep secrets from me.

But what would I have found if I did look through his phone?

CHAPTER 5

Jace's apartment smells like fresh lilacs. It's a huge step up from how it smelled when he first moved in; like motorcycle tires and pizza delivery. I set my backpack of clothing on the bench near the doorway and stretch out my arms. "This place smells amazing. I'm so glad you let me put that wax warmer in your kitchen."

"I like those wax things even if they are girly as hell." Jace locks the door behind us and hangs his keys on the key rack next to the door. I can't help but picture how one day my own car keys might get to rest on the hook next to his. He heads to the kitchen near the wax warmer and shows me a few packages of scented wax cubes that he must have bought on his own. "I used to hate these girly smells but now they just remind me of you."

"So now you like them?" I say with an *I told you so* smile. He nods. "I just like being reminded of you."

I motion toward the living room where the unmistakable changes I've made reflect off of nearly every inch of the apartment. The dark blue and grey couch pillows were bought at Target with Jace's credit card, along with the throw blankets, the fluffy rug and the welcome mat. "My presence pretty much dominates your place now," I say with a smug self-satisfaction. "What would you do without me? You'd be living like a total pig."

Jace grabs a water bottle from the refrigerator and chugs half of it. "Trust me, I live like a pig when you aren't here. I only clean up real quick before you come over."

"Ah, so the truth comes out!" I sit on the armrest of his couch and cross my arms. "Jace Adams, whatever will I do with you?"

I get lost in his smile as he approaches me. By the time I realize his look of adoration has turned into a sneaky grin, it's too late. Jace hooks an arm under my knees and around my shoulders and yanks me off the couch. I squeal and grab around his neck so I don't fall. "I've missed you so much," Jace says as he turns and walks away from the couch, carrying me with him.

Warmth floods into me as he carries me into his bedroom and gently sets me on his bed. I want to make a sarcastic comment about how he actually made his bed this time, but his lips press onto mine before I have a chance. My fingers run through his soft hair, tangling up in it since he hasn't had a haircut in a while. I shiver when his hands slide up my waist, pulling my shirt off with the help of me arching my back for him.

"Yeah," he says, gazing at my chest. "I definitely missed these." He buries his face into my cleavage and I end up giggling like a dork because his scruffy facial hair tickles.

I push his head away and he leans in for a kiss. I hold my finger up to his lips. "Not fair. If my shirt is off then yours needs to be off, too."

"Yes ma'am," he growls as he sits back on his heels while still straddling me to the bed. His arms cross in front of him and then he pulls his shirt off and I watch the ripples in his chest muscles flex as he slides the shirt over his head and tosses it to the floor. Damn, my boyfriend is hot. I press my hands to his chest, letting my fingers trail down to his abs and then hook into the waistband of his jeans. I guess my feeling him up is the girl version of him snuggling against my boobs.

We're total opposites. He thinks my squishy areas are sexy and I think his rock hard muscles are sexy. Good thing we're perfect for each other. I close my eyes as Jace showers my body with soft kisses. Shivers run across my skin as the stubble on his face tickles my hip bone.

When we're both undressed, we cuddle under the sheets and Jace makes love to me like I am the only thing in this world that matters to him. After, when I curl up in his arms and feel sleep start to fall over me, I grab on to the love I feel from my boyfriend and hold it deep inside my heart. I'm going to need it when I talk to him about moving in later.

Jace picks out the snap peas from his Chinese takeout and places them on a napkin. I reach over and grab them one by one with my chopsticks and eat them. He sticks out his tongue in disgust every time he hears them crunch in my mouth. I'd be lying if I said that wasn't half of the reason why I eat them. Jace stabs a piece of beef with his chopstick When he's hungry he doesn't bother using them in the correct way. "So have you given any more thought to what you'd like to study at the college?"

"The better question would be, 'Have you decided if you even *want* to study at the college?'" I say without bothering to hide the annoyance in my voice. I was hoping we could go at least a whole day at Jace's apartment without talking about this. I know I need to hash this out eventually but I'm perfectly fine with putting it off as long as possible.

"Why do you say that?" Jace asks. "You're not really giving college a chance. You could like it, you know."

"*You* didn't give college a chance. Why are you making me go?"

He stares straight past my head, not looking at anything but the thoughts in his own mind. "I didn't go to college because I chose a career as a professional motocross racer. That didn't exactly work out for me."

"You're doing well for yourself. You have a career that's still in motocross. I wish I had a talent that paid me a lot of money."

Jace smiles and shakes his head as he swirls his chopstick around his plate. "Oh you have talent...but I'm not going to let anyone pay you for it."

"Shut up," I say as blood rushes to my cheeks. He *so* did not bring up my bedroom skills while we're eating dinner.

When we finish eating I let Jace convince me to pull up the Brazos Community College website and browse through the different programs they offer. It's a community college and not a university so they only have two year degrees and certificate programs. Until Becca mentioned them, I had no idea what a certificate was. Turns out it's a super quick way to get certified to do various careers like the Pharmacy Technician path that Becca chose.

I skim over the list of possible careers, reading them aloud to Jace while he pours us both a drink from the kitchen. "Well?" he asks when I finish the list.

I try to stop my lip from curling. "I don't like any of these." My shoulders fall. I'm not trying to be difficult. I just can't picture myself doing any of these jobs for the rest of my life. And I'm not some stuck up girl who wants to be taken care of either. I want to work. I want to be successful and do something I'm good at and help Jace pay the bills. But for now, the only options seem to be taking a part time job in the evenings or going to college to pursue a degree in subjects I couldn't care less about.

Jace hands me a drink and settles beside me on the floor with his back resting against the couch. He looks over my shoulder at the laptop screen in my lap. "Nothing sounds good to you?" he asks. It makes me feel better since his voice isn't rude or condescending. "Maybe we should research each of the options and see what kind of jobs you can get with them. It might change your mind."

I sigh and let my head fall backward until I'm staring at the ceiling. "I wish there was a job that involved hanging out with you at the track all day."

Jace's eyes light up. "Maybe there is. I can't believe I didn't think of this earlier." He slides closer to me and asks for the laptop. I hand it over without hesitation since it belongs to him and all. With his brows furrowed in concentration, he pulls up Gmail and types in his log in information. "I'm going to email Mr. Fisher."

"Your boss? What for?"

He wiggles his eyebrows and the overly confident smile he's so good at wearing appears on his face. "I'll tell you once I know for sure."

I roll my eyes and push myself up onto the couch, stretching my feet out lengthwise. As Jace types up an email to his boss, I watch the glow of the computer screen light up his gorgeous face. Becca's words from the other day come back to me. Jace had typed in his password right in front of me without hesitation. I didn't even think to watch him type it like Becca does with the guys she dates. I wonder if he would be upset if I secretly figured out his password by spying on him as he types.

"Hey babe?" I ask, the words falling out of my mouth before my common sense can force me to shut up. "What's your email password?"

He doesn't look up from his computer. "F-M-X-5-1-9."

"Five nineteen? Aww, baby, that's the day we started dating."

Jace snorts as he continues typing the email. "Duh."

I turn to the side and rest my chin on his shoulder. "I can't believe you just told me your password."

This time he does look away from the computer. "Why wouldn't I?"

"Well…I don't know. Because it's private? Because Becca said that every guy is obsessed with keeping their stuff secret."

Jace lifts an eyebrow. "Maybe the weirdos she dates. Bay, you're my soul mate. I have no secrets from you. Everything about me is free for you to know."

"Yeah, no secrets except for talking to my mom behind my back."

He leans over and kisses me on the forehead. "That was for your own good. And trust me, she gave me no choice in the matter."

CHAPTER 6

My boyfriend's cell phone blasts the room with an annoying ringtone about thirty seconds after we finish making love. Not expecting any sounds so early in the morning, I jump, rolling backward onto the bed and losing my comfortable spot on Jace's chest.

"Perfect timing," he says as he leans toward the nightstand and grabs his phone. "It's Mr. Fisher."

I pull the comforter up to my shoulders to keep warm. Jace climbs out of bed and answers the call, not even bothering to put on any clothes. It's fine by me though, I like the view. I don't pay any attention to his phone call at first. His work stuff doesn't really concern me, not unless he's getting called into work on his day off. But then Jace turns around to face me and says, "Definitely. I'll ask Bayleigh about it. Thank you, sir."

After ending the call, Jace crawls back into bed and I reclaim my position on his chest. His arm wraps around my shoulders and squeezes my side. "So…what was that about?" I ask.

"It was about the email I sent him last night. How do you feel about administration work?"

When the smell of scrambled eggs quickly turns into the smell of scorched eggs, I hop off my barstool and shove Jace away from the stove. He wanted to be sweet and cook breakfast for us while he tells me more about this crazy work idea of his, but clearly I need to take over. He hands me the spatula with a big pouty frown on his face. "Sorry babe. I tried."

I laugh and toss the burnt eggs into the trash, then lower the heat on the stove so I can start a fresh batch. "Leave the cooking to me. You still need to finish telling me this idea of yours."

Jace grabs my butt as he walks behind me and I swat at him with the spatula. He takes a seat at the bar and continues the conversation we started in the bedroom. "Your comment about wanting to hang out at the track with me all day made me remember that Hana was looking at a stack of job applications the other day."

I crack another egg and glance back at him. "That sounds promising..." I say, more to myself than to him. Hana Fisher is the track owner's daughter and she also works at the track with Jace.

Jace taps his fingers on the counter. "Yeah, so I asked him what they were hiring for and he said they need a front desk kind of person. Someone with administration experience who can handle phone calls and paperwork and basically all the clerical stuff that goes on at the track. Jim and Hana and everyone else have a passion for the motocross aspect of it and don't like doing office stuff."

"I could totally do that," I say as thoughts of hanging out with my boyfriend at work all day play through my mind. Office stuff doesn't sound hard. I mean, I'm one hell of a copy maker and I'm quite skilled with a stapler.

"There's a catch." Jace tries to give me an innocent smile when I glance back at him. "He was only looking for someone experienced and with a college degree in administration."

I scramble the eggs with a little more force than necessary. "That's not a *catch*, Jace. That's a deal breaker. Why are you even telling me this when there's no way I could get the job?"

"Babe there's *always* a way to do *anything*."

I cut him off with a violent eye roll and shake of my head. I am not in the mood for one of his motivational speeches. I am not one of the kids he trains at the track. "And how exactly do I get a job that requires a degree when I don't have one? Do you have some kind of magic wand I don't know about?"

Sometimes I expect Jace to get angry with me when I act like this much of a bitch to him but he never does. And sometimes, like right now, his ability to remain calm makes me even more annoyed than if he had gotten mad. "Well…?" I ask after a few moments of silence.

Jace lets out a slow breath. "I'm just waiting for you to get all of your ranting over so you can be totally embarrassed when I tell you the details."

"Oh gosh," I say, already feeling my cheeks blush as I fill our plates with breakfast food that isn't burnt. "Go on."

Jace takes a huge bite of eggs and continues, "Jim likes you a lot and we all know he likes me. He said he'd be interested as hiring you as an intern while you're in college. And before you give me that look, just hear me out. There's a two year associates degree for administration. Jim said that's all you need. Once you finish that, you can get hired on fully and have benefits and vacation pay and all that."

I push the food around my plate with my fork. "That's kind of an awesome idea. I could go to college for two years. That's not too bad."

"I don't know babe." The seriousness in his voice bothers me. "It'll make your mom very happy and I know how much you hate doing that," Jace jokes with me. I stick my tongue out at him. He grabs his laptop and opens it, turning the screen toward me. "Here. You can read his email for all the details. He sounds pretty excited about getting you onboard. You know how he's all big on family and stuff."

"But I'm not family." I slide over in my barstool to read the email on his laptop.

"Yeah you are. You're my family. He knows how I feel about you."

This brings a smile to my face. "You mean he's not one of those adults who thinks we're total idiots for falling in love so early?"

Jace shakes his head. "Nope. Hana and Ash just got engaged and they're only nineteen. He's freaking psyched about it, but who can blame him? His future son-in-law is a professional motocross racer."

"Wow, they got *engaged*?" I ask, feeling a tiny tingle of jealousy pierce into me. Hana is really nice and a fun person to be around. I'm happy for her. I would love to be in her position...only with Jace and not her boyfriend. He's nice too, but a boyfriend with dreadlocks? Ew.

Jace nods with his mouth full of food. The boy has already cleaned his entire plate and I've barely touched my breakfast. He motions to the laptop for me to read. "I'm going to get dressed for work. You should look up that degree again on the BCC website and see if you'd like to do it."

An entire five minutes pass as I read the email and then check out the college's website again before I have a Becca moment and realize that I'm currently on Jace's computer with his email logged in and I have no desire to snoop around on him. I guess that's what makes Becca and me different when it comes to keeping a relationship strong.

I am not a snoop.

CHAPTER 7

Jace takes me to work with him, promising that he only has two clients to work with and that we'll get to come home by lunch time. It's sweet that he always much such an effort to get us out of there as quickly as possible; it's as if he thinks I'll get too bored and leave him. But the truth is, I love being with Jace all the time and anywhere. When he's at Mixon Motocross Park he's in his element and there is nothing sexier than watching my man hard at work.

The last time I was in his office I ended up storming out in an embarrassing display of falsely hurt feelings. I cringe just thinking about it now. A girl had come in begging Jace for extra training before a race that weekend and I stupidly thought he was blowing me off to go flirt with her. It turns out she is his cousin. At least I learned two valuable lessons that day: Jace can be trusted and I am an idiot.

When his first client arrives, I take a spot on the bleachers to watch them work. Jace typically trains a rider by standing with them on the track and giving them pointers as they ride for a lap or two and then come back to get more help. The guy he trains today must suck at turning because Jace has him practice the same two turns in the track over and over again.

A familiar face with long brown hair braided and tossed over her shoulder arrives at the bleachers. Hana waves at me with one hand while the other hand holds onto the tiny dirt bike beneath her. I think it's called a pit bike. They're slow bikes so Hana doesn't wear a helmet while riding it. She kills the engine and props it against the bottom bleacher step before climbing up to the top row to sit next to me.

She gives me a quick hug. "Hey girl, I figured you'd be back in town soon."

"Yep. School is finally over."

"Nice. You're a free woman now. So what's been up with you?"

I give her a coy smile. "I think I should be asking that of you, Miss *Ash Carter's Future Wife*."

Hana bursts into a joyful laugh and automatically shoves her hand in my lap so I can see her ring. It is absolutely stunning, and nothing less than what I would expect from Ash. The boy freaking adores her. "I'm really excited for you," I say and then I give her another hug because what the hell, I *am* really excited for her. "Have you planned a wedding date yet?"

Her lips press together in thought. "Sort of. We're having a house built and it's supposed to be done in six months. We want to time the wedding so that we can get married and then move in our house right when it's finished."

"Wow. Nineteen years old and you're already getting married and building a house." I swallow back the sting of jealousy that runs through me. "That's freaking awesome. Here I am just trying to convince myself to go to college."

Hana laughs and grabs my arm. "I'm still in shock myself. I never imagined that my life would be this awesome. Of course, we couldn't build a house if Ash hadn't gotten the professional sponsorship. I guess we're not like an average nineteen year old couple."

"Do you live with Ash now?" I ask, wondering if I'm crossing a line with the personal questions. Hana is a friend but we're not that close or anything.

She shakes her head. "We put all our money into building the house and saving for furniture and it just seemed dumb to rent an apartment for a short time. But we're together every day so it's almost like we do live together."

A kid on a dirt bike rides in front of us, revving his engine until Hana looks down at him and waves. He waves back and then zooms off. "So what are your plans for the summer?"

I tell her something simple about spending time with Jace and looking up college courses to take in the fall. I do not tell her the things that are eating away at the back of my mind because I don't know if she'll tell Jace when I'm not around. Plus it's kind of hard to express my pain over having a boyfriend who hasn't exactly asked me to live with him to a girl whose boyfriend just proposed to her.

I know I'm being pathetic, but it is what it is.

By the time Jace finishes training his second client of the day, it's well past two in the afternoon. So much for getting off work by lunch time. The extra two hours of time I spent on the bleachers after Hana had to go back to work only added to my growing depression about Jace. I couldn't stop thinking about my life and my relationship with him. Everything seemed perfect until my mother interfered with her stupid plans.

It wasn't supposed to be like this at all. Jace wasn't supposed to just *let* me live with him while I go to college—he was supposed to *ask* me to move in with him in some romantic way. We might not have talked about this specifically, but I definitely thought about it in my head for the last few months. Now I can't get over the fear that Jace is simply agreeing with Mom's plan and that he doesn't really want me with him at all. All of these thoughts haunted me this afternoon and now that I'm in the passenger seat of Jace's truck as we head back to his apartment, I can't seem to force myself to appear as if nothing is wrong.

"You okay?" Jace asks tentatively after a few moments of silence.

I nod. "Yeah."

His eyebrows wrinkle with doubt. "Are you mad that it took me longer than I promised?'

"No." It sounds like a lie, but it really isn't. I'm too consumed with thoughts about Jace to even care about how long it took him at work. It's not like I had anything else to do. It's not like I have a job or anything.

His hand reaches across the front seat, resting on my thigh with a little squeeze. "The sooner you tell me what's wrong with you, the sooner I can make it all better."

My stomach chooses this time to let out a loud growl of hunger. Jace cups his hand to his ear. "What did you say, Bayleigh's stomach? You said that Bayleigh is being a butt face for not telling me her feelings?" He nods and looks at me as if my stomach is the smartest thing in the world. "Yep, stomach. I totally agree."

This act of stupidity gets a smile out of me. Jace can be so dorky at times. He curls out his bottom lip. "Please tell me what's wrong babe."

I shake my head. "I can't tell you. It's awkward and embarrassing."

Jace pulls into the apartment parking lot and leaves the engine running.

"We're soul mates, Bay. Nothing should be awkward or embarrassing. You can tell me anything. I mean, hello!" he says, squeezing my thigh again. "I bought you tampons! I'm like the world's greatest most understanding boyfriend."

"Fine. If you really want to know then I'll tell you." I fold my arms over my chest and clench my jaw together.

"But it's going to make me look like a pathetic loser and it will probably change everything between us."

Concern dances across his features and he sits up straighter, pulling his hand away from my leg. "What's going on?"

With a sigh, I accept the red that I know will rush to my cheeks and I tell him what's on my mind. "I'm incredibly embarrassed that my mother talked to you about me living with you before I even got the chance to. It seems like you only agreed to it because you were pressured into it and I feel like you probably don't even want me to live with you. But you're too nice to admit it and the last thing I want to do is force myself to live with someone."

I can't read the emotions on my boyfriend's face. His head tilts slightly to the left as he thinks over what I just said and at one point his lips part as if he wants to say something. He looks over at me and the silence continues. Overwhelming dread floods into me at the realization that I might have just screwed things up by telling him all of this. My fingers twine together in my lap. "I'm sorry. I just didn't want things to turn out like this. I was planning on finding a job and having my own money to come down and visit you. I wanted to be a partner with you so that you would ask me to move in and I'd be able to contribute." Jace remains silent and I let my head fall as I stare at my hands. "I just feel like a burden that my mom has handed down to you. I wanted you to ask me. I never wanted to impose."

"Babe." My heart shatters at the flat tone of his voice. His face is expressionless and his mouth freezes halfway open as if he can't find anything to say. I unbuckle my seatbelt, fully ready to grab my purse and run to my car, driving back home as fast as possible.

"Just answer one question," I say as my pained heart thuds inside my chest. "Did you want me to move in this summer? Did you want things to be like this?"

Jace pulls the keys out of the ignition. He swallows. And then he looks me straight in the eyes. "No."

CHAPTER 8

The heavy metal door of Jace's truck makes a loud clink as I slam it closed. With fists clenched at my side, I sling my purse over my shoulder and power walk up the stairs to his front door. Of course I would have left my keys on the key rack inside his apartment. Of course I couldn't have been smart enough to keep them in my purse in case I needed to make a quick escape!

Of freaking course!

The front door isn't locked and I throw myself inside while the sound of Jace's footsteps slowly ascend the stairs behind me. I grab my keys and swoop around, ready to make a break for my car and hoping that he won't stop me on the stairway.

My hope is in vain because of course he does stop me. Jace's muscular frame stands in the middle of the metal staircase. His hands grasp onto either side of the railing; a silent way of telling me that I won't be going anywhere anytime soon. I glance over the edge and briefly consider taking a leap of faith over the railing. But we're about ten feet in the air and I'm not sure I can drive home if my ankles are shattered.

I turn back to Jace. "Let me leave."

"Is that what you really want?"

I can't look into his eyes so I glance away. "Yes."

Jace takes one step forward, one step closer to me. He's a few stairs below me so I'm the taller one. I use this opportunity to peer down at him, trying to strengthen my confidence. I will not break in front of Jace. I will not let him see me be weak. "This was obviously a mistake. I'm not staying here with you if you don't feel the same way that I do. Please let me leave."

"Maybe I misunderstood," Jace says, taking one more step closer to me. "But I thought we were a couple who could talk about things. I listened to your thoughts in my truck back there. Now it's time for you to listen to mine."

I tighten my jaw and he takes another step forward, making us eye to eye on the staircase now. "I think you owe me that."

With no other option but to retreat, I turn and walk back into the apartment, dropping my purse on the couch and sitting next to it. I place my hands in my lap and give him my undivided attention. "I'm ready to listen."

Jace ignores me and slips inside his bedroom for a few seconds that seem to last an awkwardly long time. When he returns, he walks right in front of me and sits on the coffee table, facing me. He holds out a red envelope that has my name written on it. The handwriting is Jace's, but by the looks of the elegant cursive lettering and the smiley face at the bottom, he put some thought into it making it not look like his usual chicken scratch.

I take the envelope and slide my finger under the seal. "Are you breaking up with me in a greeting card?"

"No, this is the card I planned to give you on our anniversary next Saturday."

"Why are you giving it to me early?"

He shrugs. "Because it's the only way I can think of that will make you believe me when I tell you what I have to say."

Intrigued, and still a bit heartbroken at his earlier confession, I slide out the card and skim the words on the front. It's a poem about love and spending a year together and other sappy things. When I open the card, something shiny catches my attention. Taped to the inside of the card is a silver house key. Chills prickle up my arms.

Under the key is a handwritten note from Jace:

The second key I gave you was to your car.

The third key I'm giving you is to my apartment, which I hope will become our home.

In case you're wondering about the first key, it's the key to my heart and you've had it since day one. Happy first anniversary Bay.

I love you always,

Jace

I blink back tears as I pull at the tape that holds the key to the card. "Why did you say no in the truck just now?"

Jace reaches forward and grabs my hands, folding the key into the middle of my palm. "I said no when you asked if I wanted things to be like the way they are now. No, I didn't want your mom to corner me and force me to go along with her plan for your future. No, I didn't want you forced into moving in with me when I didn't know if you wanted to or not. I don't like things the way they are now. I wanted it to be different."

"Me too," I mumble. His words had just somehow managed to stitch together the broken pieces of my heart, but I'm still not wholly happy again. Things are still weird. "So why didn't you just ask me to move in with you? Who cares what my mom thinks or wants?"

He glances at the card. "I *was* going to ask! I was waiting until our anniversary for obvious romantic reasons. Your mom just jumped the gun and I wasn't going to ignore her. I kind of had no chance but to along with her."

I lean forward and wrap my arms around his neck. His hands slide around my back and he pulls me onto his lap on the coffee table. "I love you Bayleigh. You are my entire life. I want to spend every single second with you."

"I want to spend every second with you," I whisper while my head rests on his shoulder. "I'm sorry I ruined your anniversary present."

"No worries." His voice is peppy and a little cocky. I lean back and look at him just in time to see his sly smile. "We will have tons more anniversaries and you can't possibly ruin them all."

CHAPTER 9

The sun beats down on us from the top row of bleachers at Mixon Motocross Park. Becca pulls out her hair tie, throws her head back and gathers up all of her hair again piling it into a messy bun on the top of her head. "This place is so freaking hot. How do you put up with this?"

I hand her an opened water bottle from the cooler at my feet but she doesn't grab it right away because she's distracted by the shirtless guy in board shorts who makes his way up the bleachers. He stops halfway up and takes a seat to watch the races. "Never mind. Now I see how you deal with the heat."

"Eh, that guy is a prick." I skim the crowd for Jace who should be back any minute now with our nachos but I can't find him. "There are tons of other hot guys here who would be worth dating."

Becca fans her face with her hand. "Hook me up girl, damn."

When Jace finally returns, balancing three orders of nachos in his hands, he has Hana Fisher with him. Before I ravenously dig into my nachos I make sure to introduce her to Becca since they've both heard so much about each other.

"Hana has something to tell you," Jace says, grabbing one of the cheese-less chips out of my basket and eating it for me. The boy knows I hate the chips unless they're drenched in gooey and delicious fake cheese product.

"What's that?" I ask.

Hana's excitement makes her bounce up and down where she sits. "So you know how my dad was having a pool built in his backyard? It's finally done and Ash and I are throwing a huge pool party this Saturday. We want you to come. Becca, you should come too."

"Count me in," Becca replies instantly, her eyes still on the shirtless hottie a few seats below us.

"That sounds great," I say, right as realization hits me. I turn to Jace. "This Saturday is our…thing." I don't know how to end the sentence because we haven't exactly made plans for our anniversary, we just know that we want to do something.

"It's up to you babe."

I gnaw on my bottom lip. "The party sounds really fun…" Jace laughs and steals another one of my chips.

"Then let's go to the party. It'll be more fun than a romantic dinner."

My excitement for the pool party and our anniversary has me smiling on the whole drive back home where I plan on packing up as much of my things as I can fit into my car. I'm not officially moved in with Jace yet, but we both decided to make it a gradual transition to where I will end up being moved in with him before my mother even knows what's happened. It will all work out though because I'm definitely going to college so that I can work with Jace.

In the end, I think that's all Mom really wants to see from me.

My bedroom smells stale since I haven't lived in it all week. I grab all the bags and backpacks I own and begin stuffing them with clothes. Remembering the pool party, I dig through my top drawer and retrieve the brand new bikini I purchased last year and never got the chance to wear because I was stuck at my grandparent's house all summer. It's white with rhinestone decorations. I toss it in my bag and then head over to my desk to grab my checkbook, extra phone charger, a bottle of daily vitamins and my day planner.

Shit. My day planner. My fingers tremble with the shocking realization of something that could totally ruin my weekend. How could I have forgotten what time of the month it was? I flip open the planner to today's date and all the breath escapes my lungs.

My palm slams into my forehead. Friday is the start of period week. The week of cramps and bloating and tampons. Ugh! Why?! Why *this* week of all weeks? Why on my anniversary and why on the night of the pool party where my only bathing suit is a freaking white bikini? So much for having a great one year anniversary with Jace.

I'll have to spend the night hanging out poolside in shorts and a t-shirt instead of swimming with my hot boyfriend and letting him feel me up under the water. I know they say you can swim while wearing a tampon but with my craptastic luck, I am so not going to risk it. The last thing I need is to climb out of the pool gushing blood in front of dozens of horrified onlookers.

I shudder at the thought. And then I grab the few remaining tampons I have and head back to Jace's apartment. Becca had to leave Jace's earlier today to attend her grandma's birthday party so even though I try calling her to vent about my period problem, she doesn't answer. Not having anyone to talk to leaves me driving the entire forty-five minutes to Mixon all by myself. I'm stuck inside my own head and all I can do is freak out about how my stupid body and its stupid menstrual cycle is going to mess up my one year celebration.

And it's not just one day either. It's an entire week. Ugh! I don't even know how I'm going to explain it to Jace. I mean, he's not an idiot. He knows that girls have periods. I've just been lucky enough to not have to talk to him about it in the entire year we've been together. He's always had to travel for work during those times or I've stayed home and used an excuse of homework and school projects to avoid seeing him for those five days. But now that we will be living together, it's a fact of life that I'll have to face.

My knuckles grip the steering wheel. Oh well. As mortified as I am to talk to Jace about girly stuff, I know he'll be cool with it. He's cool with everything else that happens between us. That's what makes him the world's greatest boyfriend.

I couldn't be more proud to be his girlfriend.

CHAPTER 10

My stomach bulges as I swallow down the last few bites of my third slice of pizza. I lick the grease off my fingers and then place a hand on my belly. "If we're going to live together we need to learn how to cook real food."

"This is real food," Jace mumbles through a mouthful of cheese and pepperoni.

"I mean home cooked food. You order takeout like every day. At this rate I'm gonna get super fat and you'll leave me."

Jace snorts and rolls his eyes. "I'm never leaving you."

"Oh yeah?" I stand up from the couch and shove my stomach out as far as it'll go. Then I lean forward and press it against his face while he watches television. "What if I get super fat?"

"If you get super fat then I'll get super fat." He swallows my food and kisses my stomach. "But we can cook more if you want. I guess I can't live the bachelor lifestyle forever."

I ruffle his hair on my way into the kitchen to get a drink. "You're damn right you can't. You're a committed man now. You have to put up with me and all of my quirks."

Jace laughs from the living room. "Bring it."

Once again I've found myself in a situation where I could easily bring up the topic of periods and the other topic of how I'll be getting mine so and ruining our anniversary. And once again, I just stand awkwardly with my mouth halfway open, trying to force the words out of my mouth. Every time I try though, I just freeze up and change the subject. It is so freaking awkward telling a guy something like that.

Knots form in my stomach because I know I can't keep putting it off. I'm supposed to start either tonight or tomorrow. He will know something is up the moment I refuse to sleep with him. Come on, Bayleigh. It's not that bad! *Just tell him!*

"Hellooo," Jace singsongs while waving at me. "Why are you staring off into space?"

I flinch, realizing I had been caught up in my own thoughts too long, and take a seat next to Jace. "Sorry, I was just…thinking."

"About what?"

Once again, this is the perfect opportunity to tell him. But I'm a total chicken. "Um, about school."

"Have you decided on the summer class?"

"Yeah, I think so." Jace smiles when he hears my answer. I'm happy too, although school isn't even on my mind right now. Yesterday I had gone to the college and spoke with a counselor who helped me get admitted and pick out my classes for the next semester. I can even start earlier than the fall by taking a summer class. Things are looking really freaking awesome for my future.

Soon I'll be in school, then I'll be finished with school and I'll get to work full time with Jace. We can stay in Mixon and maybe buy a house after he sells his grandfather's house that's a couple hours away in Salt Gap, Texas. We can live happily ever after together. Happy thoughts of the future help me take my mind off of the inevitable for a few hours longer.

I'll tell him eventually. I'll have to.

After a hot shower, I climb into bed with Jace at a little past midnight. His arm wraps around me as I snuggle against his chest, feeling lighter because I still haven't started my monthly annoyingness. So when

Jace's calloused hands slide down my belly, I let him pull off my pajamas. I guess I'll tell him tomorrow.

CHAPTER 11

The smell of coffee wakes me up the next morning. Well, the smell of coffee and the loud, "Dammit!" from my boyfriend who tripped over something on his way into our bedroom. I sit up on my elbow and rub my eyes open. The bright sunlight streaming in from the window he just opened burns my vision with its morning goodness. "What's going on?" I ask, squinting as my eyes adjust to the daylight.

Jace wears just a pair of black boxers as he enters the room carrying a wooden tray. "Happy Anniversary beautiful."

My eyes graze over his sculpted chest before noticing the tray. "Babe! You brought me breakfast in bed?" My excitement turns into confusion as he sits next to me, placing the tray between us. "I mean…coffee in bed," I say with another smile. The tray contains two coffee mugs, one with regular coffee for Jace and the other he has prepared just for me: topped with whipped cream and chocolate sprinkles.

Jace leans over to kiss me and I make an effort to keep my lips closed because of the morning breath. "This is just to wake us up. I'm taking you to Star Diner for breakfast."

I take a sip of coffee and lick the whipped cream off my lips. "What's Star Diner?"

He gives me a sneaky smile. "You will love it. I promise."

The drive to the illusive Star Diner takes almost an hour. Long trips with Jace aren't so bad though. Time seems to magically skip ahead when I'm with him. We arrive at a small town along the coast and he's so freaking excited about showing me the diner, I almost expect him to make me close my eyes so it'll be more of a surprise.

The only parking available is along the street and Jace and I dig around his truck for enough change to fill the parking meter. We hold hands as we walk along the strip of businesses toward the massive metal sign that says "Star Diner – since 1906."

My eyes light up and I glance over at Jace who squeezes my hand. "Remember when you said you wished you could experience one of those old fashioned soda fountains?" he asks.

I nod as we approach the old metal doors and he holds it open for me. "Well, I found one. Today we're going to get breakfast and an old fashioned milkshake."

My enthusiasm for an old fashioned soda fountain drops to negative levels the moment we walk in the door. Although everything in the diner is straight from the early twentieth century, our waitress is clearly from this century. And she can't contain her excitement about who just entered her workplace.

The beautiful woman in a short black skirt and red tights who looks to be in her late twenties escorts us to the bar where we take a seat on a red leather barstool. "Oh my god, it's Jace Adams!"

He answers her and it doesn't really bother me at first. I've heard those words a million times when I'm out in public with him. His answer is always yes and then we have to pause for a quick photo or autograph and then the star-struck stranger goes about their way and that's that. Looks like that won't be happening today.

Our waitress's name is Julie and I know that not because she told us, but because I read it on her nametag.

After she hands us menus, she doesn't take our drink order or walk away—nope, she plops herself down on the barstool on the other side of Jace and begins chatting with him like they're old friends.

And I don't mean that as an expression. She actually sounds like they're old friends. I look up from skimming my menu and watch their conversation.

"So then James had to quit because of his ankle injury and I think they didn't ask him to come back."

"Wow," Jace says as he looks over his menu. "That's too bad. James was a good rider."

Maybe he knows her from the motocross world. Mixon isn't that far away and people travel from all over the state to race there. I shrug off the feeling in my chest and look back at my menu. And then I overhear her say something that really rubs me the wrong way.

"So what's been up with you? Why can't you answer emails anymore?"

My body freezes. My eyes blur until the words on the menu don't make any sense to me. The seconds between her question and Jace's answer seem to stretch on for an eternity and all I can do is sit here pretending that I'm not eavesdropping.

When Jace finally answers, I don't feel any better at all. "Oh you know. I've been crazy busy with work."

"If you're so busy, why are you showing up here instead of working?" Her eyebrows shoot to the ceiling and she hooks her hand on her hip as if daring him to answer.

Jace laughs and then throws an arm around my shoulders. "I blew off work to take my girlfriend here for breakfast. She loves old fashioned places like this."

Oh wow, did Jace remember he actually has a girlfriend? I think sarcastically as the girl gives me a quick smile of acknowledgement and I return the gesture. "I'm ready to order," I say, keeping my voice strong so she can't tell that their conversation has turned me into a jealous PMS-ing monster.

I order the French toast with bacon and Jace does too. When she finally freaking leaves, sashaying her perfectly round butt as she greets the elderly couple that arrives next, I cross my arms over my chest and sigh.

"What's wrong?" Jace asks, nudging me with his shoulder as he pours several packets of sugar into his iced tea.

"Nothing," I say. "I love when girls approach you and talk about how you haven't been replying to their emails."

"Babe…" Jace begins but I cut him off.

"Save it," I hiss under my breath because we're seated just opposite of the guy cooking our food in the middle of the bar. "I'd rather not know why you two have a history."

He slides his hand around my back and I stiffen, not accepting his affectionate touch. "It's not like that."

I look him in the eyes and try to hold back the tears that form in mine. "I'm trying not to get jealous here but you know a million girls and they're all attractive and they all look at you like you're some kind of sex god."

He wiggles his eyebrows. "I am a sex god. But only for you."

I smile despite myself. "That doesn't make me feel any better."

"Well it should. You're the only girl who means anything to me."

The drive home takes longer than usual since I'm no longer in happy-happy romance road trip mood with Jace. Sure, I smile and laugh at his jokes and participate in the conversation about how fun the pool party will be tonight, but inside I'm a total mess. The worst part is that I'm not even mad at Jace. That would be stupid. I'm mad at myself for how insanely jealous I get over things that are not a big deal. Jace is allowed to have friends. Hell, he's allowed to have ex-girlfriends. I have ex-boyfriends! But I seriously need to learn to chill out and stop worrying about silly things like this.

So what if a girl complained that he hasn't replied to her emails? That's a good thing. It's way better than if she had said, "Thanks for all your long heartfelt emails that you send every day!"

I can't help but roll my eyes as I think up such ridiculous scenarios. Jace must notice my odd facial expression because he turns down the radio. "What's going on in your head? You look like you're insanely deep in thought. Like…so deep that you might slip into a coma or something."

I roll my eyes again, this time directing my sarcasm toward him. "I'm just excited for tonight." The moment the words are out of my mouth I realize how incredibly untrue they are. I am so not excited about spending the afternoon in a white bikini being too nervous to swim because of personal embarrassing girly problems. I still haven't started though, so maybe I won't start until tomorrow. Maybe I didn't track the days on my calendar well enough and maybe I'm off by a few days. I was caught up in the excitement of graduating last month. For all I know, my period could be due next week instead of this one.

"I'm not excited," Jace says. "My hot ass girlfriend walking around a bunch of guys in a bikini?" He takes his hand off the steering wheel to wave a fist in the air. "I'll be spending the whole night beating up guys for checking you out."

"You're dumb," I say with a laugh. "But...you actually reminded me of something." My heartbeat quickens. I know what I'm about to do and I'm so nervous I could explode.

"What's that?"

I swallow and look over at him. Wait, scratch that. I look over at the seatbelt crossed over his chest. I can't possibly look directly at him as I say this. "I'm supposed to have certain...girly problems...soon. So I might not get to wear that bikini after all."

His reply is the worst possible reply ever.

"Huh?"

I take a deep breath and think of another way to explain my situation. "You know…the monthly thing that girls suffer through? I'm expecting mine soon."

"Ah," he says in a moment of realization. My palms are so sweaty and my throat feels dry from all the effort it took to say that. And now that it's out in the open, I don't feel much better. I'm still mortified beyond belief. Jace doesn't seem embarrassed though. He shrugs. "Well that works out perfectly. I won't have to kick anyone's ass for checking out your hot body."

I look over and meet his eyes and he winks. Heat flushes to my cheeks as overwhelming reassuring warmth spreads through my body. I finally told Jace what I needed to tell him. The hard part is over.

Now if only I could stop thinking about that stupid waitress.

CHAPTER 12

After breakfast, Jace has to make a quick trip to the motocross track to help his boss sort out some paperwork crisis for next week's race. Normally I don't like spending time away from him but right now I could use a break and some best friend time so I stay at the apartment and call Becca. She answers on the fifth ring.

"You better not be calling to tell me the party has been cancelled because I just spent eighty bucks on a bathing suit."

I consider lying and telling her it has been cancelled just to see how long she'll freak out. "No, I just need to vent for a moment."

"Holy crap, is there trouble in Jace and Bayleigh's perfect paradise?"

I let out a breath. "Yeah. Only Jace's paradise is still perfect."

Becca listens to me tell her what happened with the waitress like a true friend—by staying quiet until I'm finished with every last crazy obsessive worry I unload on her.

"So?" she says as she piles all of her stuff into her car and prepares to make the drive over here. "You know what you need to do now."

I peek through the curtains in the living room on the off chance that Jace has returned home early. "I do?"

"Duh! Check his emails, girl. Find out exactly what that skank waitress has been emailing him about."

"There's no way I can do that. That's an invasion of privacy."

The sound of her blowing a raspberry with her tongue filters through the phone. "He gave you his password. It's not an invasion. If anything, it's an invitation."

"I dunno," I say, turning around and glancing to where his laptop rests on the kitchen counter. "It just feels wrong."

"Fiiiiiine, Miss Upstandingly Moral. Just try to log in with the password he gave you. If he didn't want you to see her emails then he would have changed the password."

She makes a good point. One that I can't seem to find a way to shut down. I toy over the idea in my head for the rest of our conversation. She tells me the directions she pulled off of the internet from her house to Jace's apartment to make sure they're right because this is the first time she'll be driving herself to Mixon. I tell her she's good to go, but in reality I have no idea if her directions were correct or not.

I'm still mentally stuck on the email thing.

Once we're off the phone and I've double, triple and quadruple checked the parking lot for Jace's truck, not to mention sending him a text asking him to call me when he's on his way home, I sneak over to the laptop in the kitchen. My pulse races and my hands actually shake as I take the laptop, open it and turn it on. An overwhelming feeling of embarrassment consumes me as I click on the browser and then go to Jace's email screen.

I don't even need to use the password he gave me because it's already logged in. That means he didn't change it and he doesn't have anything to hide. I suck in a deep breath and take one step backward from the computer, glancing out the front window again and finding Jace's parking spot still empty. Well, that's it I guess. The password wasn't changed and that's all I wanted to know.

A few seconds later, I'm typing the letters J-U-L-I-E into the email search bar and I'm feeling like a total snoopy asshole for doing it. But then I hit enter and brace myself for the results.

More than a dozen emails from one Julie Garner show up on the screen. I knew they would, but the knowledge doesn't stop the ball of bitter anxiety that swells up in my throat. The most recent email was received nine months ago. He didn't reply to it. Nor to the three before that one. I should feel relief, but I don't because Jace and I were dating nine months ago. The idea of a girl emailing him, even if he didn't reply, just kills me.

I know I'll regret it, but I click on the first email and skim the contents. They aren't so bad. Just random stuff about work and motocross—well that's good news. A tiny voice in the back of my mind tells me to close the email, turn off the computer and put it back right freaking now! I've already snooped more than I ever should have and I didn't find anything bad.

But I don't listen to that little voice. I click on the next one. And the next one.

My eyes blur with a mixture of hurt and anger and other emotions I don't even comprehend right now.

A picture of her wearing a skintight dress and posing with her hand on her hip next to another equally beautiful girl.

...come on Jace I know you aren't my boyfriend but you're like my best friend...

...how come you never reply to me anymore? You didn't even say anything about my picture!...

Sad face. Sad face. Sad face.

I'm clicking through emails like a mad woman now, skimming random lines in her long emails before moving on to the next one.

Click. Click. Click.

Stop.

Panic.

On June 11th of last year, Julie Garner sent an email to Jace that didn't contain a single word. Just a picture of herself, naked and spread eagle on a bed.

Now I really do click out of the email and close the laptop. Now I really do put it back where I found it in the kitchen.

I don't want to do the math in my head, to trace back the dates and figure out when exactly she sent him that picture. But I do it anyway. Jace and I started dating on May 19th. It doesn't take a math genius to know that June comes right after that.

The knot in my stomach rises up into my throat. I make it to the bathroom just in time to empty the contents of my stomach in one acidy, disgusting hurl. My eyes squeeze shut as I hover over the toilet puking out my guts. Amidst everything, the puke and the vile stench of it and the horrid taste in my mouth, all I can think about is one thing—Julie Garner's perfectly shaped naked body.

It's way more beautiful than I'll ever be.

CHAPTER 13

A loud knock on the front door makes me jump out of my thoughts and land back in the real world. Somehow I ended up on the bathroom floor, knees pulled to my chest with tears streaming down my face. The knock comes again, this time more forceful. It's right about now that I notice my cell phone is ringing from the other room.

I jump up and wipe the tears off my face with the back of my hand. My stomach fills with nausea but I ignore it and pull open the front door. To my relief, it's Becca and not Jace. Not that I have any desire to see anyone at the moment, but my best friend is a whole lot better than Jace.

"Good god what is wrong with you?" Becca yanks off her sunglasses and tosses them onto the floor with her purse and a beach bag. She's already wearing her eighty dollar bikini under a pink sundress and she smells faintly of self-tanner. "Have you been crying? What is that smell?"

My face crumples in confusion because nothing she says makes any sense right now. All I can think about is

Julie's perfect boobs and the fact that Jace saw them. He could look at that email every day for all I know.

Becca's arms wrap around me as I burst into tears and fall to my knees. She drops to the floor and asks me a million questions. Finally something snaps me out of my insanity. "Should I call 9-1-1? What is it Bayleigh, you're freaking me the hell out!"

I look up and swallow, blinking back tears. I shake my head and sniffle until I can breathe again. "No. No I'm fine. I'm just…heartbroken." My voice cracks at that last word and my eyes threaten to gush out tears again. Becca grabs my wrists and squeezes them tightly in my lap.

Her words are precise and spoken slowly as if I'm a child with a hearing impairment. "What. The. Hell. Happened?"

I take a deep breath. "I read Jace's email."

Her eyes practically bulge out of her skull. "And?" she says with as much calmness as she can possibly muster. I know it's taking every ounce of energy in her body not to freak out and beg for every dirty little detail. Luckily for her, she doesn't have to beg.

I tell her absolutely everything I found and she listens with her eyes wide and her hand over her open mouth. "Wait, that was sent nine months ago?"

I nod. "Yeah but we were dating nine months ago."

She gnaws on her bottom lip and rocks back on her heels. "Girl... I don't know. I mean, this is bad but it isn't *bad*, bad. You know?"

I blink and a stray tear trails down my cheek. I can tell she's struggling to find the right words to say; probably searching for a lie that will make me feel better. Well good luck because it's not going to work. "Okay look." She takes a deep breath and puts on her Serious Face. "He didn't reply to the emails. You had to search for it so it's not like had it saved as a favorite or anything. Plus, we both know he's hella famous and girls probably throw themselves at him all the time. Hell, I bet he has tons of naked photos from other girls trying to get his attention."

My calm façade cracks into a million pieces again. "Thanks a lot. You didn't have to put more worries in my mind."

"Ugh, I'm sorry. I shouldn't have said that. Look Bayleigh, it's going to be okay. Jace isn't cheating on you and he never has. Some crazy bitch emailed him looking for attention. Screw her."

"You're right," I say with a renewed feeling of strength. "He hasn't cheated on me, so it's not the worst thing in the world. I just feel like I know something that I shouldn't have ever known. I've seen something I shouldn't have seen. I'm ruined now."

A million thoughts and worries swarm around my mind. How many times did Jace look at that picture? How many more pictures have girls sent him? Does he ever think about her when we're together? But somehow, my love for him and for what we have together still hangs on, desperate to make things work. "How am I ever going to come back from this? How am I going to forget that I saw anything and go on with my life?"

Becca's head tilts sideways and her lips squish to the left. "Maybe you should talk to Jace about it. Get his explanation."

"There's no way in hell that's happening." My hand shoots to my stomach as another wave of nausea hits me. "Just thinking about it makes me want to throw up again."

"Again? Girl go brush your teeth. Your breath smells like something died in there."

The front door swings open and we both jump. Jace walks inside while staring at his cell phone. When he sees us sitting on the floor, his expression goes from calm to anxious. "Babe? What's wrong? Have you been crying?"

I open my mouth to reply but Becca beats me to it. "The girl tripped over her own feet and crashed into the coffee table. She's fine though so don't get any closer. We were just on our way to get all pretty for the pool party." She grabs my wrist and pulls me off the floor. "So no peeking!"

"Okay but you two are weird," Jace says as he heads into the kitchen to get a drink. Becca pulls me down the hallway toward Jace's bedroom. "I love you Bay," he calls out.

"I love you too," I yell back, hoping to god that my voice doesn't sound as shattered as I feel.

Becca forces me to brush my teeth and wash my face. The fresh breath and cool water splashing on my face helps pull me out of my funk. I have to put on a happy face after all. It's my one year anniversary and I'll be spending it with dozens of other people at a friend's house.

Happy thoughts.

Must think happy thoughts.

Must pretend to be as happy as you were before you knew the things you aren't supposed to know.

"There's no point in wearing makeup." I give Becca a judgmental sideways glance as she applies eyeliner in front of the mirror. "It's a pool party. All that shit will just wash off."

"But what if I meet a hot motocross guy before I get in the water?" She stops talking to open her mouth as she carefully applies the eyeliner. "I'm sure the place will be packed with hot guys and I'm not missing out on that opportunity."

I laugh and for one tiny fraction of a second I've completely forgotten the stupid photo. Then it comes back to me full force, punching me in the face as if to say *screw you, I'm not letting you forget about me!*

I hide behind the closet door as I slip into my bikini and pull a pair of jean shorts on over it. I chose the darkest pair of shorts I have just to provide period protection if my dreaded monthly curse decides to finally show up in the middle of the party.

With my terrible luck, it probably will. It'll be a perfect end to a perfectly horrible day.

"Hey, I have to ask you something and you can't tell anyone about this at all for the rest of your life." I give Becca my Super Serious Face so she knows I'm not kidding.

She cocks and eyebrow. "As if the entire last thirty minutes weren't already a secret?" she asks.

"Good point." I sit on the bed and watch her finish applying her makeup. "Yeah so, I'm wearing a white bathing suit because it's the only one I have and I'm gonna need you to…okay I know this is gross, but I need you to be my official backup because I might be getting my period soon."

"You mean you want me to check out your ass occasionally to make sure you haven't bled everywhere?"

"You don't have to be so damn blunt about it," I say with an awkward laugh. "But yeah."

"If you're about to be on the rag why the hell would you even go to a pool party? With a white bathing suit?"

I shrug. "I'm not entirely sure I'm about to start. I was supposed to start a few days ago but I haven't yet so I'm thinking maybe I miscalculated on my calendar."

Becca replaces the cap on her mascara and slowly puts the tube back into her makeup case. When she looks at me her face is completely blank.

"What? Am I totally stupid for risking it tonight? I'm not cramping or anything so I don't think it'll happen at the party."

"Bayleigh, you might have a bigger problem than some skank's naked photos."

"What does that mean?" I ask it even though I'm already putting together the puzzle in my mind. A sharp stab of terror pierces my heart.

Becca sits next to me on the bed. "Don't you see? You've been crying like a lunatic over finding a silly email from nine months ago. That is so not like you. You're a hormonal freak right now. What if you're pregnant? Oh my god what if you're pregnant?"

Her words hang in the air as silence envelopes us. I think about crying or screaming or jumping into denial mode. I could pace the room or crumple into a ball on the floor. But I don't do anything. It's as if my brain has reached maximum thinking capacity and locked up, unable to function anymore.

Jace appears in the doorway. "How much longer until you girls are ready?"

Becca puts her hand on my shoulder and gives me a look as if to tell me that all I need to do is give her a sign and she'll take over from here. I shrug her off and stand up.

"We're done," I say. "Let's go."

CHAPTER 14

Becca tries to be a supportive friend by sticking to my side at the pool party when Jace is pulled away to talk motocross politics with his boss and other coworkers. But when Hana's fiancé introduces us to a group of twenty year old muscular motocross racers, I put on a carefree smile and tell her she should follow them into the hot tub.

"No way, I'm not leaving you," she says, but the way her eyes follow the guy's backsides as they walk away tells me she's already mentally gone anyhow.

"Please do," I say, giving her a little shove in that direction. "I'm fine, really."

"I don't know…" she hesitates.

I make my smile more convincing. Hell, my fake smile has reached such convincing proportions maybe I'll start to believe it. "Go. I'm grateful for your help but you drove all the way out here and I'm not going to make you suffer just for my sake."

"Okay but I'm here if you need me."

"I know."

Hana and Ash take turns pushing each other off a donut-shaped pool toy in the middle of the water. My boyfriend is still stuck talking with his boss and although I could go stand with him, I'm afraid someone will ask me something and I'll be too emotionally distraught to answer. So I head to the shallow end of the pool and sit on the edge, letting my bare feet dangle in the water. I lean back on my palms, tilting my face toward the sky as I pretend to soak up the last remaining rays of sunshine.

The fear of possibly being pregnant weighs heavily on my mind. Out of both terrible things that happened to me today, it's completely obvious that my late period is the one I should be worried about. Those stupid emails happened months ago and my late period is happening right now. But I can't let the emails go.

I can't stop thinking about the very real fact that my boyfriend has naked photos of another girl on his computer. Why would he bother giving me a key to his apartment if he still has stuff like that from his past? Why would he plan a future with me and convince me to go to college and arrange a job at the track if he still has girls on the side?

Oh god. My stomach, which may or may not be implanted with Jace's child, tightens into a painful knot. If I'm pregnant then I can kiss my future goodbye. My future job, my education...none of it is attainable if I have to raise a baby.

I glance up from the pool and lock eyes with Jace. He's all the way across the backyard but I think he smiles at me. I can't be sure. All I know is that I can't be here anymore. All of these happy people with their carefree lives and their stupid laughter that keeps getting louder. People don't cry at pool parties and that's exactly what I'll do if I stay here any longer.

I push myself up from the edge of the pool and slide my sandals on, not even bothering to dry off my feet. I don't glance at Jace and I don't look for Becca.

I just run.

Hana's house is next door to the motocross track. I'm all the way through the thin line of trees that separate the two and crossing over the wooden bridge that enters into the park by the time I start to run out of breath. Dirt sticks to my wet feet and rubs painfully inside my sandals but I keep running anyhow. I don't look back. No one calls my name or runs after me. I doubt anyone noticed that I left.

The sun begins to fade, dipping behind the trees at the edge of the motocross track. My legs slow to a walk and then my body stops completely. This place is creepy at dusk. All the massive dirt jumps are shadowed and transformed into eerie lurking monsters. The massive metal bleachers look uninviting and scary without any people around.

I sit on a sawed off tree stump in the middle of the grassy area where people park their cars during a race. My heart still thumps away under my chest, trying to calm down from the rush of hurt and fear and exercise I just put it through. My face sinks into my hands and I stare at the dirt on my feet, watching as it morphs into blurry shapes under the tears that fall from my eyes.

Why am I even out here? What the hell am I doing?

"Bayleigh!"

The unexpected sound startles me but I don't look up because I'd know that voice anywhere. Footsteps get closer and faster as Jace jogs toward me. He doesn't say anything else and I feel his body brush against mine a second later. He sits next to me on the tree stump. We're silent for a moment.

"Becca said I needed to talk to you."

I look up. My eyes meet his and I can't tell what sort of emotion he hides behind his blank expression. "What else did she tell you?"

He blinks. "She said it wasn't her secret to tell."

I decide to stare at my hands instead of at my boyfriend. I'm not even sure he will still want to be my boyfriend after he finds out what I have to say. "Secrets."

"What?"

"Secrets," I repeat. "Plural. There are two of them."

"Wow." He runs a hand through his hair. "And here I thought everything was fine."

I snort in spite of myself. How lucky he must be to live his life thinking things are just fine and freaking dandy. Jace turns toward me and takes my hand. "You need to talk. Now."

What are the rules for telling your boyfriend two very awful things? Do you tell him the least awful one first or the most awful one first? How do you even decide which is the worst? The possible pregnancy, obviously.

I mean, I guess?

If I'm not pregnant then the emails are the worst thing. I'm not sure I can stay with a guy who keeps emails like that despite having a girlfriend. I'm also not sure Jace would stay with me if I got pregnant. Either way, the odds of my relationship staying together after tonight seem slim to none.

"You're doing it again," he says.

"Doing what?"

He brushes the hair out of my eyes. "Thinking. You've got some kind of crazy monologue going on in your head and you're too busy telling it to yourself to tell it to me. Talk to me, Bay. You didn't run out here by yourself for nothing. What's going on?"

I draw in a deep breath. It's now or never I guess.

Although *never* sounds like a pretty great choice.

Without trying to be mean, I slide my hand out of his grasp. I'm not sure he'll want to be touching me when I tell him my secrets. This weird desire to kiss him falls over me and I restrain myself. Now is so not the time.

In one breath I tell him everything—the faster and quicker I get it out, the better. "My period is several days late and Becca said I might be pregnant and I also snooped in your emails and saw Julie's freaking naked body and messages about how you're not her boyfriend and she wants you to be and I can't live with the guilt of knowing what I know." When the words are out, I don't feel relief. I don't feel much of anything.

Jace stiffens. "What all did you see in my email?"

"I searched her name and I didn't read them all…I just read enough to know that she likes. And she sent you naked pictures, Jace. And you didn't delete them." My voice is one shattered, shaking mess.

Jace leans forward, concern stitched across his face. "You didn't read any other emails? Nothing recent?"

My brows knit together. "What? No." More heartache and confusion grip me, making breathing difficult. What doesn't he want me to know? What could possibly be worse than Julie's photo? "What else is on your email?" I ask as tears fill my eyes. "What else didn't I see?"

"No, nothing" he breaths, wrapping his arms around my shoulders and pulling me in close to him. He squeezes so hard I can't breathe. "Thank god."

I push him off of me and stand up. "What the hell, Jace? This isn't a good thing. What else is in your email?"

He smiles. What an asshole. I'm crying my eyes out and he *smiles*? "It's nothing bad. I'm just glad you didn't see it."

My hands ball into fists at my sides. "Screw you, Jace. How dare you smile about this!"

His hand reaches out to me but I step backward. "I'm sorry baby. I didn't mean to smile. Honey, it's…I'm sorry you saw her emails but I swear I forgot they were there. I didn't look at her skanky picture, I promise you."

"How the hell am I supposed to believe that?" I ask.

"Because I wouldn't lie to you. Look, just sit down and I'll explain." He pats the tree stump next to him and I shake my head. "I'd rather stand, thanks."

My anger levels soften as I listen to Jace explain himself about Julie. He says that she used to date one of his friends and they all hung out a lot. After his friend broke up with her (because she was a little crazy), Julie started flirting with Jace but he never flirted back because he didn't like her. He said he was nice to her because she was psycho and then her emails became more and more obsessive and his only option was to ignore her.

"So she just sent you that photo out of nowhere?" I ask, my hands on my hips. "You didn't ask her to send it?"

"God no." His face crumples up in revulsion. "I actually remember that day. I was driving to your house and I opened the email at a red light. The second I saw the photo, I called her and bitched her out and said not to send that shit again. If you read the emails right after that one, she apologized and said she was sorry. Did you see that part?"

I shake my head. Relief floods over me but I'm still disappointed. "Why didn't you delete the email? You should have had more respect for me."

"I know, baby and I'm sorry. Honestly I just forgot about it. I get like a hundred work emails a day and they pile up and I never saw it again." This time when he reaches for my hand, I take it. "Please believe me, Bay. I will delete every email from her tonight, I promise."

I let him pull me into his lap and the rush of emotions I feel when I lay my head against his chest comfort me in ways I haven't felt lately. This is Jace. My

Jace. He feels like home to me and I hate when things aren't right with us. "Um…babe?" I ask, as I snuggle my face into his neck. "Did you not…um…pay attention to the first part I said?"

He shrugs. "That you might be pregnant?" He says it so casually you'd think I just ask him if he heard me ask what time it is. "Uh, yeah," I say sarcastically. "I mean, I hope it's not the case, but I don't know and..I—"

Jace's finger covers my lips. "I think we'd make awesome parents, so whatever happens, happens. Don't you agree?"

I pull back and look at him, my eyes wide with curiosity. "Are you serious?"

"Yes ma'am."

"You wouldn't get mad and leave me?"

"I'd die before I'd leave you."

With that, my heart bursts into a thousand pieces. I slide my arms around his neck and pull him into me, inhaling the intoxicating scent of his cologne and embracing the way his shaggy hair feels against my cheek.

Jace lets out a sigh. He taps my thigh. "I need to stand up for a minute."

Confused, I get off his lap and sit alone on the stump. Jace's expression gets a little weird as he stands up and pulls his phone out of his pocket. "Bayleigh..." he says, as if whatever he has to tell me is causing him a great deal of effort to spit out. His face lights up from the glow of his cell phone. "The reason I was worried that you saw my recent emails is...well, shit maybe this isn't the right time to tell you."

"Uh, you bet your ass it's the right time to tell me. You can't just say something like that and then not finish it."

He smiles as his finger slides around on the phone screen. He clicks on an email and then holds it out to me, but the words are too small for me to read so I just look at him expectantly, waiting an explanation. "My newest emails are from the owner of KC Jewels. The last thing I want is for you to see the emails and ruin the surprise, but... hell I guess I'm ruining it already. Bay, I wasn't at the track earlier today when I left you at home."

I gnaw on my lower lip as he continues. "I was at the jewelry shop, seeing the progress they've made on the custom engagement ring I designed for you. It won't be ready for a couple more days but he sent me a picture of what it will look like," he explains as he turns the phone back around to face me. My mouth falls open at the amazing hand sketched image of a gorgeous diamond ring with filigree accent diamonds along the band.

It takes a moment for what he's saying to sink in. I mean, I know what the words 'custom engagement ring' mean but it takes a while for my brain to register the reason why Jace is suddenly dropping down on one knee.

Under the twilight of an empty motocross park and with the glowing of his cell phone reflecting off our faces, Jace holds out the phone to me as if it were a ring box and takes my hand. "Bayleigh. The last three hundred and sixty five days have been the most amazing part of my entire life. Will you..." he blinks and one tear rolls down his cheek. "Will you...pretend this is a real ring and not a cell phone and do me the honor of being my wife?"

"Yes, baby I will." I drop to my knees in front of him and throw my arms around his neck. He lets the phone fall to the ground as we collide and land in the soft grass. I kiss him as tears roll down my cheeks. Jace brushes the hair out of my face and kisses me back. He tastes like Vanilla Dr. Pepper. It's never felt so good to be in his arms. None of the things I worried about feel like worries anymore. The feeling of his hands holding me tightly to him lets me know that whatever happens, we're in this together.

"I'm yours forever," he whispers into my ear. "For this year, and every year for the rest of our lives."

His promise makes me warm and happy inside. All the shattered pieces of my heart mend themselves back together and an overwhelming feeling of peace falls over me as we lie on the grass and look up at the dark sky. I don't know if I'm pregnant or not, but I do know one thing.

I don't ever want this night to end.

The End

NOTE FROM THE AUTHOR

I wrote Summer Unplugged over the course of several Mondays while I waited for my daughter to get out of dance class. I wasn't sure anyone would like the characters I created or care about their story, but I wrote it anyway because they made me happy. To my surprise, not even twenty four hours after Summer Unplugged was published, I had readers emailing me asking if there would be more books.

And just like that, the Summer Unplugged Series was born. I hope you enjoyed following Jace and Bayleigh's journey and I want to sincerely thank you for sticking with them until the end. Every email, Tweet and Facebook comment I get from readers means so much to me as an author.

You guys have inspired me to continue writing new series with new characters and new love stories. I hope you will enjoy them as well.

Thank you for your support!

Never stop reading! <3

ABOUT THE AUTHOR

Amy Sparling is a Texas native with a passion for young adult literature. In her free time she participates in an unhealthy amount of Xbox playing, attends nerd conventions and reads books with her daughter. Amy Sparling is a pen name for author Cheyanne Young.

You can tweet her @Amy_Sparling or visit her at www.AmySparling.com

If you would like to be the first to know about new releases from Amy, please sign up for her mailing list here: https://tinyletter.com/AmySparling

Made in the USA
Lexington, KY
17 December 2014